The Butterfly

By Judith

with Mark S

Illustrated by Ben and Tina Garrison

ISBN 1-880812-17-7

10 9 8 7 6

Published by Storytellers Ink
Seattle, Washington

Printed in Mexico

Contents

Chapter 1

A New Adventure

Jerry had to pass the old house every morning on his way to school. Some people called it the haunted house. No one had lived there for a long time and the windows and doors were boarded over. Jerry thought it would be too scary to go inside, anyway. The yard had grown into a jungle because there was nobody to cut the weeds or prune the bushes. It really looked like a haunted house to Jerry, and now he could see that it was going to be torn down.

A yellow plastic ribbon wound around the whole yard to keep people out of danger. Two big orange trucks waited at the curb next to a bulldozer. Three construction workers in hard hats stood talking to each other in front of the house. They were making plans about how to do the job.

Jerry stood near the yellow ribbon to watch. One of the construction workers climbed up on the huge bulldozer. When he started it up it made a noise like a fierce monster waking up.

Jerry sat down in the weeds along the sidewalk, almost underneath the yellow ribbon. The grass and wildflowers were so tall they were almost over his head. They smelled dry and made his nose itch. He pulled off one of the long blades of grass to chew on. He had to make a decision. It was getting close to school time. It would be so cool to see the house torn down, though.

The bulldozer backed off of its trailer into the street and then turned and climbed straight up the curb, onto the front yard. Jerry hoped it would keep going and smash the house. But the bulldozer stopped when it got near the house, and the driver shut it off and got down. Then all the construction workers disappeared around the side of the house.

Jerry lay back in the grass and looked straight up into the sky. There were no clouds at all, just blue and more blue, with a circle of weeds that stretched up all around him. He would know when the driver came back to the bull-dozer because it would make a lot of noise when he started it.

Jerry knew he was cutting it close. He knew that school would begin soon. But he couldn't tear himself away. This was where the fun was. Looking at new things, exploring his favorite places, finding adventures, that's what Jerry loved most. Sometimes it got him into trouble. He never complained when he had to stay after school or clean the chalkboards. He knew that this was the price he paid for his adventures. Today, he really wanted to see the bulldozer knock down the old house.

Jerry stopped daydreaming when he noticed a tiny black dot in the sky. It dropped slowly toward him from what seemed like a mile high. He kept his eye on the dot and it got bigger and bigger. As it came closer he saw that it was a butterfly, fluttering lower and lower in lazy circles.

Finally, it landed on one of the weeds just above his head. Now he could see every part of it. It had beautiful orange wings with black veins running through them, and feelers stretching out from its little head. It was using its feelers to inspect the leaf of the plant it had landed on, balancing delicately as the leaf moved slightly in the breeze. Jerry tried to stay very still.

The butterfly checked out the leaf very carefully. It walked to the edge of the leaf, then to the underside of it. He wondered how it could hold on upside-down like that. It didn't seem to have claws or stickers or anything that he could see. While he was wondering about this, the butterfly did something that amazed Jerry. It crouched down and left one tiny, perfect, white egg on the leaf.

"Wow, awesome!" Jerry whispered to himself. The mother butterfly walked back over the top of the leaf. She moved toward another leaf. Just then, the bulldozer rattled to life with a huge bang. Startled, the mother butterfly flitted up and away.

Jerry sat up to see what was going on. The bulldozer wasn't starting in on the house yet. It was cutting a path through the yard. One of the construction workers came up to Jerry.

"Better move back, kid," he yelled over the noise of the big machine.

"Aren't you guys gonna tear down the house?" Jerry asked.

"Not for a while. Sorry," he said. Jerry could see the bulldozer working back and forth across the yard, leveling row after row of weeds. He thought of the butterfly mother, her one tiny egg on the leaf beside him. What would happen to it? He reached down and pulled up the plant. He was very careful not to jiggle the leaf and knock off the egg.

"See ya," he called to the construction worker.

"Bye!" he yelled back, waving. Jerry threw his backpack over his shoulder and grabbed the leaf where it connected to the stem of the plant. He turned the leaf so that the egg was on the top, and tried to keep it perfectly still all the way to school.

Chapter 2

The Deal

Jerry could hear the first bell from a block away. He knew he would be in trouble. He slipped through the door of his classroom and walked very quickly to his desk, not looking at Mrs. King.

"Jerry?"

"Yes, Mrs. King?"

"Do you have an excuse for being tardy?" she asked.

"Well, I left home really early this morning, Mrs. King, but then I saw some construction workers with a bulldozer. They were going to knock down the haunted house, and I stopped for just a minute to watch. And then...."

"It's your job to be on time for school, Jerry. You know that."

"Yes, Ma'am, I know that. But I thought I could see the house crash down and still run to school in time."

"Did they knock it down?" she asked.

"No, ma'am, not yet. But you see, I was waiting for them to smash the house, and I looked up and saw this big butterfly."

"So the butterfly made you late, Jerry?" He heard a few giggles.

"Well, sort of," Jerry explained. "I was waiting in the long grass for the bulldozer. They were tearing up all the weeds in the yard. And then this butterfly landed on this leaf next to me. And she, well, I think she laid an egg." Everyone laughed.

"What's so funny?" Mrs. King asked the rest of the class. Neil spoke up.

"Oh, right, like a little tiny butterfly can lay an egg like a chicken. What are you going to do, Jerry, make scrambled eggs?" The kids laughed again.

"Neil, not all eggs are like chicken eggs," Mrs. King said and frowned. Jerry felt better. He held up the weed and pointed to the leaf.

"There," he said; "there's her egg." The little white egg was so small it was hard to see.

"Where?" Jefferson said. "I don't see it."

"It's really tiny. Look." Jerry held it up so Jefferson could get a good look.

"What makes you think that tiny white dot is an egg?" he said.

"I'm telling you, I saw her. She landed on the top of the leaf. She sniffed around with her feelers. Then she walked underneath and laid this one egg before the bulldozer scared her away. I thought the egg would be lost when they plowed the yard. So I brought it with me." Some of the kids were out of their seats as they tried to see the tiny egg.

"I see it," Melissa said.

"I do too," agreed Danny. He was standing in the aisle.

Mrs. King said, "All right, class. Stay in your seats. Jerry, please put the plant on the back shelf. We will discuss this at recess."

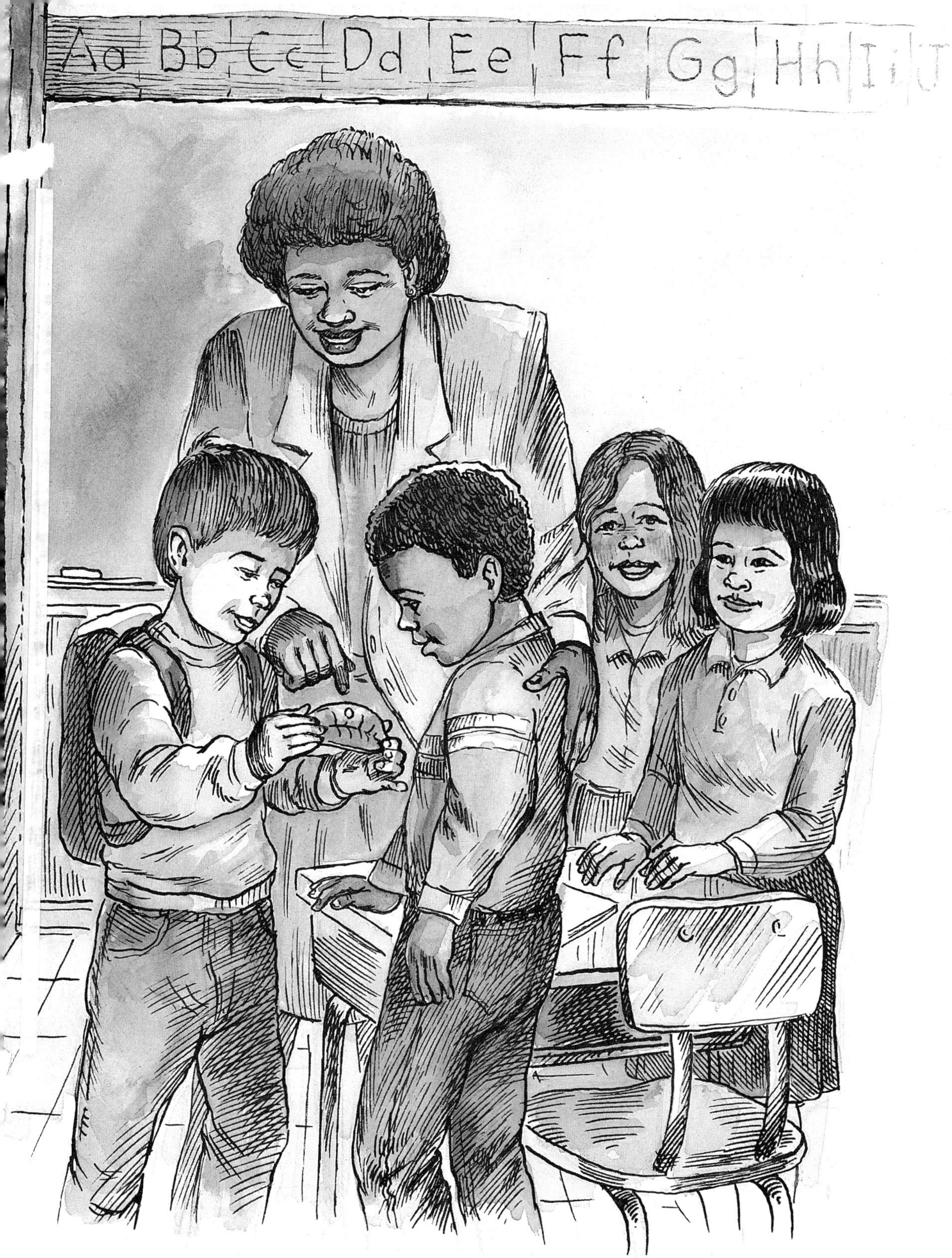
Aa Bb Cc Dd Ee Ff Gg Hh Ii J

"Yes, ma'am," Jerry said. He went to the back of the room and set the milkweed on the counter. Then he returned to his seat.

When the recess bell rang Mrs. King said, "Jerry, please come here for a moment." Jerry went to the chair next to her desk and sat down. He tried to sit up straight. Jerry liked Mrs. King. She was a strict teacher, but very fair.

"I thought maybe we could work out a deal, Jerry," Mrs. King said.

"Like what, Mrs. King?" he asked.

"Well, you could stay after school and clean the chalkboards for being late, or you could stay after and do something about your butterfly egg instead." Jerry smiled. "After school, why don't you get a box from Mr. Yellin and set up a place for your egg by the window. Then go to the library and look for a book about butterflies. See if you can identify the kind you saw."

"Sure, Mrs. King. That sounds fun."

"But you have to promise me something. You need to remember that being on time for school is very important. Do you think you can try harder to be on time?"

"Okay, I promise, Mrs. King. I don't want to be late. It seems like things just happen."

"Well, please try to think ahead so you can be on time every single morning. Now, go join the class at recess," she said, smiling.

That afternoon, Jerry got a box from the janitor. He lined the bottom of the box with grass, and put the weed with its tiny egg inside.

It was harder to find the book in the school library than he thought. He had to ask the librarian for help. Finally, they found a book with pages and pages of colored pictures of all the different butterflies and their names. He checked it out and took it home with him.

On the way home, he passed the place where the haunted house had been.
Nothing was left but a flat, smooth, dirt yard; not a board, weed, or piece of
old sidewalk was left.

Chapter 3
A Visitor

The next morning, Jerry was glad to be at his desk on time because the first thing that Mrs. King did was to introduce a visitor to the class.

"Class, this is Mrs. Levicoff."

"You can call me the Butterfly Lady, children," she said with a smile. "I hear someone watched a butterfly lay an egg yesterday." Jerry raised his hand.

"Yes, Ma'am. I did. I think it was a Monarch butterfly. The egg is right over there." He pointed to his box in the window.

"Why do you think it was a Monarch?" the Butterfly Lady asked.

"Because it was orange and black and big, and the pattern on its wing looked like the pictures in this book," Jerry said, and he handed her the library book.

"Good work, Jerry. You're right!" Jerry looked at Mrs. King and she winked at him. The Butterfly Lady began to tell the class a story about the life of a Monarch butterfly.

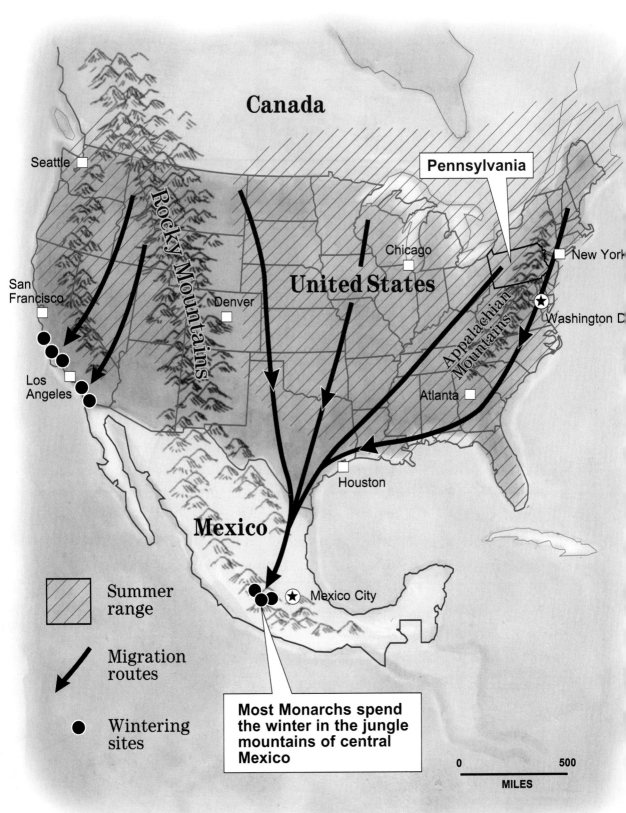

Seattle

Canada

Rocky Mountains

San Francisco

Denver

United States

Chicago

Pennsylvania

New York

Washington D

Appalachian Mountains

Los Angeles

Atlanta

Houston

Mexico

Mexico City

Summer range

Migration routes

Wintering sites

Most Monarchs spend the winter in the jungle mountains of central Mexico

0   500

MILES

"The mother butterfly who laid your egg probably came from Mexico. Like many other Monarchs, she had to fly more than two thousand miles just to lay that egg here in Pennsylvania."

"All the newly hatched butterflies grow up to have babies of their own, and this goes on for about five generations until the end of summer.

"In the fall, the great, great grandchildren who have never been there suddenly take off for the jungle mountains of Mexico. When they arrive, they look for a tree called the Oyamel tree."

Jerry raised his hand. "They're so small," he said. "And they can't fly very fast. An airplane can fly a whole lot faster."

"That's true. That's what makes it so amazing. In one day they can travel over one-hundred miles."

"They can fly as high as ten-thousand feet," the Butterfly Lady continued. "They may be little, but they're very determined. A really big mystery is how they know where Mexico is."

The class was surprised that butterflies could fly to Mexico, but they still weren't sure why they did. The Butterfly Lady explained, "They're looking for just the right habitat. A habitat is an environment every creature, even a person, needs in order to live."

"So is a habitat like a neighborhood?" Ahmed asked.

"Yes, in a way. A Monarch butterfly needs several different neighbor-hoods. It needs the warm winters in the Mexican mountains and the summers here in Pennsylvania, with lots of blooming flowers. It especially needs a plant called milkweed."

Everyone in class knew what milkweed was. It had a pod with silky threads inside and sticky white juice.

"Milkweed is where they always lay their eggs," said the Butterfly Lady. "That's milkweed that you have in your box. The mother butterfly was flying around looking for that plant. When her babies hatch out of their eggs they are called larvae. Larvae need the leaves of the milkweed to eat and grow, and it makes them poisonous to predators. It's the only thing that will keep them alive. The butterflies have to go to places where milkweed grows.

"But what happens if the Oyamel trees they need in Mexico, or the milkweed plants they need here are cut down? Well, their habitat is ruined and they have no way to keep themselves alive. It isn't so hard for people to live in a different place, but butterflies can't do it. That's why it's important for us to try to keep their habitats, their neighborhoods, safe."

"That's what happened at the haunted house." Jerry said. "The construction workers had to clean up the lot. They thought the yard was just a bunch of weeds and stuff. They didn't know that butterflies need milkweed."

"Yes. They probably didn't know. Some things that look useless to people may be very important to animals and insects. But now that you know, what do you think we can do to help, and why is it important for us to help the butterflies?"

"We'd have to find some more milkweed, I guess," Jerry said.

"They're pretty to watch, and if they all died we wouldn't be able to look at them," volunteered Mary Beth.

"Yes," the Butterfly Lady said. "The earth would be a less attractive place to live without butterflies, but there's an even more important reason. They help make the air we breathe and the food we eat."

"When the butterfly lands on a flower to sip the nectar which is its food, the flower's pollen sticks to its legs and is transferred to the next flower it visits. This allows the plants to reproduce themselves, and produce some of the oxygen for us to breathe. The pollen also helps the plant produce the fruit we eat. The butterfly needs the flowers to survive, and the flowers need the butterfly to help create new flowers. Everyone and everything in a habitat is important. Each depends on the others. "

"Monarchs need milkweed and flowers to live so they can help us live?" Jerry asked. Then he remembered the bulldozer. "What if there isn't enough milkweed or flowers for them?"

The Butterfly Lady smiled. "What could we do about that, class?"

"Plant milkweeds."

"Plant flowers."

"Yes, that's good;" the Butterfly Lady was pleased. "We could make another habitat. It could be a butterfly garden, where they would be safe to play and eat, and lay their eggs."

"Oh, yes, let's do that!" exclaimed Judy. Jerry and the rest of the class nodded in agreement.

"Well, I have a few things here to help you get started." The Butterfly Lady reached into her bag. She brought out a small glass jar with a piece of netting over the opening. Inside were two yellow, black and white caterpillars. "These are from my garden at home." Everyone leaned forward to look. "I'll pass this around." She handed the jar to José in the first row.

"These caterpillars were tiny eggs once. Just like the one Jerry found. When did the mother lay the egg, Jerry?"

"Yesterday," he said.

"It takes about three days for them to hatch," the Butterfly Lady said, "so keep a close eye on it tomorrow. The little baby that comes out won't be a butterfly. It's called a larva. The larva needs to eat to grow and get strong just like we do.

"The larva eats milkweed leaves. Then it grows into a caterpillar that looks like the ones in the jar. The caterpillar keeps eating milkweed. It's the only food it can eat in this stage. It eats so much its skin gets tight and there isn't room for any more food.

"Then something amazing happens. The skin splits open and there's a new skin underneath.

24

"The caterpillar has to change its small skin for a larger one so it can keep growing larger."

"All this work makes the caterpillar hungrier. So it starts to eat again. And guess what it eats?"

Everybody could guess. "More milkweed!"

The Butterfly Lady smiled. "Yes. The young caterpillar eats so much that it increases in weight almost 2,700 times. How much would you weigh if you were a nine pound baby and you grew 2,700 times? Over twelve tons! In the next two weeks the caterpillar has to change its skin and color four more times."

"Finally, the yellow, black and white caterpillar doesn't want any more milkweed, and is ready for the really big change. It needs to attach itself to a strong twig for the next stage of its development.

"The caterpillar hangs upside-down in the shape of a 'J', and its skin splits one last time; it looks like a jade green jewel. This is called a chrysalis. The caterpillar lives here for two weeks while its body goes through the final change.

"The chrysalis is like a tent that protects the caterpillar from wind, rain and enemies. When it is about to hatch it turns almost black, and you can look through it to see the new life inside.

"When the chrysalis splits open, as if by magic, the striped caterpillar is gone. Now it's a beautiful orange, black and white Monarch butterfly. Just like the one Jerry saw yesterday. The young butterfly is hungry, but it doesn't eat the leaves of the milkweed. Instead, it sips nectar from the flowers of that plant, and others.

"With your help, these caterpillars in my jar will become butterflies soon. They'll live for five weeks and as we now know, their great, great grandchildren will fly all the way to Mexico. Would you like to plant a garden for them?" asked the Butterfly Lady.

"Yes!" The children cheered.

Chapter 4

Changes

Mrs. King found a perfect spot near the playground that was sunny all day, and the Butterfly Lady brought asters, zinnia, bluebells, goldenrod and lots of milkweed to plant. Everybody helped.

Then they put the caterpillars in the box with the egg, added some milkweed leaves, covered the top with a screen and put it in the middle of the garden.

Mrs. King suggested that the class start a diary. Each day they would note everything that happened. Had the egg hatched? Was the larva eating? Had the caterpillars built chrysalises?

The caterpillars that the Butterfly Lady brought seemed to do nothing but eat. They used their front three pairs of legs to hold onto a leaf. Then they chewed and chewed and chewed. They had five other pairs of legs called claspers. They used these to hold onto a stem while they reached for a leaf.

Four days later, when Jerry arrived at school Carrie rushed over.

"Jerry, I can't find the egg. Wasn't it on this leaf?" Jerry looked down at the leaf.

"Yeah, I'm sure it was." Then he realized there were three caterpillars in the box instead of two. The third one was tiny with a black head. It was chewing away on a leaf.

"I think it's called a larva when it's that small," Carrie said. "They have to get bigger and have stripes. Then they are real caterpillars."

"Hello, little larva," Jerry said. "I'm Jerry and this is Carrie."

"Jerry, a larva doesn't understand English," Carrie said.

"Who knows," Jerry grinned. "Maybe you just have to teach them when they're real young. Holá, habla Español?"

"It doesn't speak Spanish, either," Carrie giggled.

Over the next two weeks, the older caterpillars shed their skins four more times. The little one did, too, a few days behind the others.

Soon the two older caterpillars climbed to the top of the box. They were hanging upside-down in the shape of a 'J'.

"They're turning into chrysalises, and now their skin is supposed to become like a house," Jerry said.

"Not a house," Carrie said, "it's a chrysalis."

"Well, even if you call it a chrysalis, they still live in it," Jerry said. "And when they come out, they'll be butterflies."

"Wow, that's cool," Neil said. Everyone nodded. It was amazing to think that those caterpillars with all those legs were going to come out of the chrysalises with wings and fly.

"Come on, little one," Jerry said to the one he had brought to class as a tiny egg. "You have to catch up to the rest of your family."

"Look," Ben said, pointing. The caterpillars' skin was splitting and sliding up. Mrs. King joined them to watch.

Two days later, Jerry hurried to school. He rushed to the butterfly box. None of the other kids had arrived yet.

"Yeah! The caterpillar did it!" Jerry was excited. The one he thought of as his caterpillar was hanging upside-down. The chrysalis was around it. It had appeared over night like magic. He wanted to touch it, to feel the casing.

Jerry carefully lifted the screen. He tried to keep his arm still. He did not want the chrysalis to fall off.

He reached up very carefully and softly touched the chrysalis.

"Jerry! What are you doing?" Carrie was standing right behind him. He hadn't heard anyone come in. Her voice startled him, and his finger slipped and pressed against the side of the chrysalis. He set the screen back down.

"Carrie, you scared me. I just wanted to see what it felt like," he told her.

"It could have fallen off the twig," she said.

"I was careful," Jerry said. But he was feeling a little guilty.

33

For two weeks the class took turns watching the chrysalises. Then one morning Mitchell shouted, "Hey look! They did it!"

The rest of the class crowded around the box. There in the place of one of the chrysalises was a beautiful orange and black butterfly, standing on a milkweed leaf. They were silent as they watched in admiration. Finally, someone said, "Let's name it."

"Is it a boy or a girl?" Carrie asked.

"Hah," said Neil. "You can't tell a boy butterfly from a girl butterfly."

"It's a boy," Jerry said loudly. He didn't like Neil to tease Carrie.

"How do you know, Butterfly Man?" joked Neil.

"It has a big black spot right there," Jerry pointed out. "And it has another one on the other lower wing. The boys have that spot. Girl butterflies don't. That's what the book says."

Then something began to happen with the second, older chrysalis. It began to wriggle. The butterfly wrapped inside was struggling to be born. A crack appeared. It got wider. And slowly, another butterfly came out.

"Cool," Neil whispered. The new butterfly unrolled its wings. It waved them slowly.

"Look," Devlin said, "no spots. It's a girl. Maybe we should call them Fred and Wilma, or Bert and Ernie."

"But one has to be a girl's name," Melissa said, "so how about Michael and Meryl?"

"Michael and Meryl? Where did that come from?" Jorge asked.

"I just thought it up. They both begin with 'M' like Monarch. Michael and Meryl Monarch. It sounds good," Melissa said.

Mrs. King said, "All right, those are good names, but now that they are butterflies they need nectar. We'll put a pot of flowers in there for them until they move outside. Now, back to your seats. We have work to do."

The children headed back to their desks. Jerry stayed behind. He leaned close to the last chrysalis and whispered, "I hope you're okay in there."

Chapter 5
Challenges

On Monday morning Carrie was looking at the butterflies. There were still a few minutes until class began. Then she went up to Mrs. King's desk, whispered something to her, and the two of them went back over to look at the box. Everyone got very quiet.

When Jerry saw Mrs. King at the box, he began to feel nervous.

"Come and have a look, class. We have a new butterfly."

"It's a girl," Carrie said. "But something is wrong. She has only one wing." It was true. The butterfly gently waved her wing back and forth, but everyone could see that she would never be able to fly like her brother and sister.

"It's my fault," Jerry said.

"Why, Jerry?" Mrs. King asked.

"I didn't mean to hurt it, but I touched the chrysalis. I shouldn't have done it," Jerry said.

"Well, curiosity can be a good thing. But you must be careful and think about what you're doing before experimenting."

"I'll try. I never meant to hurt her."

"It's okay," Jerry heard someone say.

"She'll be all right," Carrie said. Jerry felt a little better.

"I'm sure you didn't mean to hurt her," Mrs. King said. "We can't even be sure that's why she only has one wing. Maybe there's another reason. Besides, you saved her life. Having one wing doesn't mean she won't be happy. She will just be different from the other butterflies. She's special. And now I think we should give her a name."

"It should start with an 'M'. How about Mary? Or Maddie? Or Mollie? Hey, yeah, Mollie. Mollie Monarch," Carrie said.

"Michael, Meryl, and Mollie. Sounds good to me," said Mrs. King.

Chapter 6
Free

On the last day of school, the Butterfly Lady came to help them release Michael and Meryl. The whole class gathered around the box.

"They're going to love the garden you've made for them. Are you ready to take them out?" she asked. Jerry spoke up.

"Mollie has only one wing. She can't fly like the others or take care of herself. We've watched her so far, but no one will be here in the summer."

The Butterfly Lady looked closely at Mollie. She was on the petal of a flower. "A one-winged butterfly. I've never seen one before. I'll tell you what. I have a butterfly garden at my house. I'll take her home with me and look after her there." The children were relieved.

"Shall we take her brother and sister outside now?" The Butterfly Lady lifted the screen and scooped Michael and Meryl into a net. The class followed her outside to the garden. She opened the net, and up they flew. The class clapped and cheered.

All the kids watched Michael and Meryl flying around the garden until they settled on flowers to drink nectar.

"Enjoy your garden, Michael and Meryl. And don't worry about your sister. I'll take good care of her," the Butterfly Lady said.

It was time for her to leave. Mrs. King asked Jerry to help the Butterfly Lady load her things into her car. He got Mollie's box and carried it out. She opened the car door for him, and Jerry set it down.

"Maybe you can't fly, but you are a special butterfly. Not many butterflies get to ride in a car," Jerry told her.

"Don't worry, Jerry. She will have a beautiful garden full of flowers to live in." The Butterfly Lady smiled."Why don't you come and visit her this summer?"

"Thanks, and thanks a lot for taking care of her," Jerry said.

"No trouble at all," she said and got in her car. "Goodbye, Jerry."

"Bye." He waved as the Butterfly Lady drove Mollie out of the parking lot and towards her new garden.

Jerry did go to visit that summer. He found Mollie drinking nectar for breakfast. She sat in the sun all day long, drank from beautiful flowers, and played with all sorts of other butterflies that lived there. She could not join the others in flying around the garden, but she was the only one who was taken inside the house. The Butterfly Lady brought her in every night to keep her warm and safe. Jerry knew Mollie's life was different, but she seemed happy. He was glad to have been a part of the journey that brought her to the butterfly garden.